DEC - 2 2004
P9-ASM-354
3 1479 00427 1945

Haverhill Public Library
Founded 1874
Haverhill, Massachusetts

MARIAN E. BOUTIN FUND

Suddenly ALLIGATOR

Gratefully, to Bill, Wendy, Tylor, Alisha, Zachary, and Christian Walton —R. W.

To my beautiful wife Debbie whose selfless support got me through the endless hours, weekends, and late nights working on this project —J. B.

First Edition
08 07 06 05 04 5 4 3 2 1

Text ©2004 Rick Walton
Illustrations ©2004 Jim Bradshaw

All rights reserved. No part of this book may be reproduced by any means whatsoever without written permission from the publisher, except brief portions quoted for purpose of review.

Published by
Gibbs Smith, Publisher
P.O. Box 667
Layton, Utah 84041

1.800.748.5439 orders
www.gibbs-smith.com

Designed and produced by Jim Bradshaw
Printed and bound in Hong Kong

Library of Congress Cataloging-in-Publication Data
Walton, Rick.
Suddenly, alligator! : an adverbial tale / Rick Walton ; illustrations by Jim Bradshaw.—1st ed.
p. cm.
Summary: While on his way to buy new socks to replace those he has been wearing for three months, a boy runs into a hungry alligator and finds that his old socks come in handy.
ISBN 1-58685-313-9
[1. Socks—Fiction. 2. Alligators—Fiction.] I. Bradshaw, Jim, ill. II. Title.
PZ7.W1774Su 2004
[E]—dc22 2004004528

Written by Rick Walton

Suddenly Alligator

An Adverbial Tale

Haverhill Public Library
99 Main Street
Haverhill, Mass 01830

Illustrated by Jim Bradshaw

GIBBS SMITH
Gibbs Smith, Publisher
Salt Lake City

I had worn the same pair of socks for three months. Whenever I took off my shoes, the smell made my head spin **dizzily.**

It was time to buy a new pair. I headed to town. I took the scenic route, through the swamp. I was in no hurry. I walked **lazily.**

I wasn't far into the swamp when I saw it. In the mud. Hard and white. Gleaming **silently.**

My golf ball! So that's where I'd hit it. I picked it up and put it into my right pocket **gratefully.**

I walked on. What was that? Something long and green? Could it be, I asked myself **anxiously?**

gulp!

Yes! My rusty bugle. I slung
it over my shoulder happily.

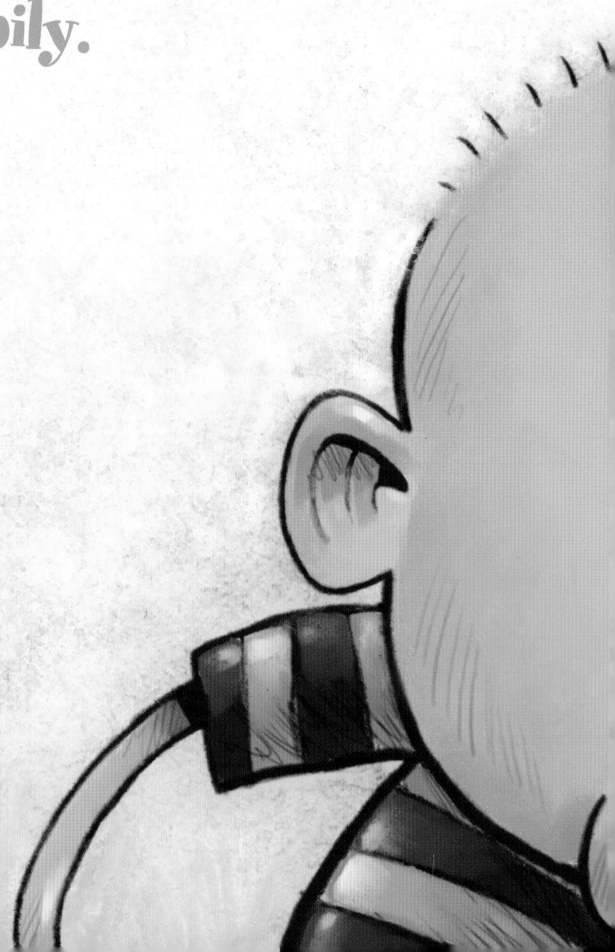

And then . . . over there . . . A big mouth
full of teeth. I approached cautiously.
easy does it...

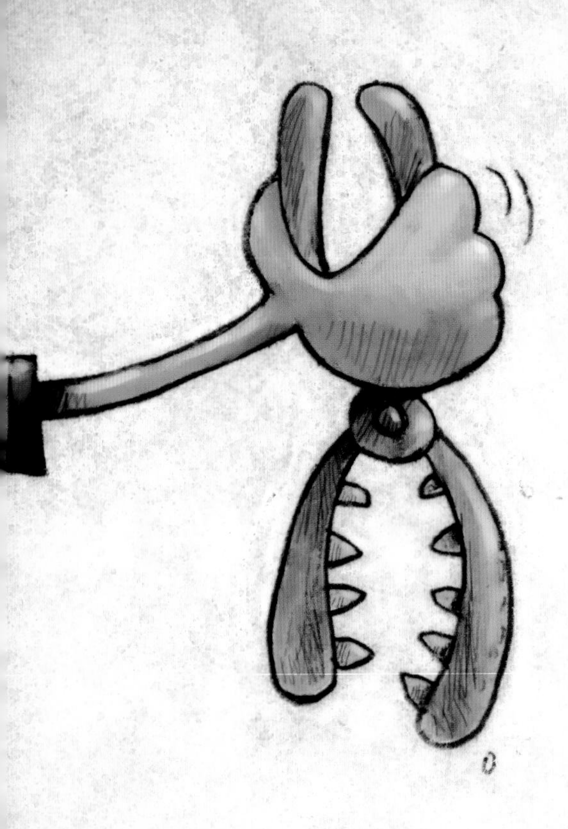

My dad's pliers! So that's where
I'd dropped them. Dad would be happy.
I picked them up and slipped them
into my left pocket easily.

I kept walking. I stepped over a stream. I stepped over another stream. And then I stepped cheerfully...

GROooooo! GROoooooo!
gulp!

… over an alligator! “Grooo! Grooo!” He flipped his tail and knocked my legs out from under me. I fell into the water. The alligator smiled at me **hungrily.**

GROOOOOOOOOO!

I decided I'd rather not be eaten. I got up and ran for the hill. Alligators don't climb hills, I thought. Ahead of me the hill rose **steeply.**

When I reached the top I stopped and turned around. "Grooo!" There was the alligator! He wasn't supposed to be there. He snapped at me. I jumped. He missed me. **Barely.**

I ran down the other side of the hill. Over logs. Around rocks. Through streams. The alligator followed me steadily.

At last I'd had enough. I stopped. I turned. "Leave me alone!" I stomped my foot angrily.

But the alligator didn't stop. He kept coming. I pulled the bugle off my shoulder and blew it **boldly.**

BON

The alligator was not afraid. I reached in my pocket. I pulled out the golf ball. I threw it. It hit the alligator on the nose. The alligator growled and came at me even more **swiftly.**

I turned again and ran. He nipped at my heels with his razor-sharp teeth. I pulled out the pliers. Perhaps I could remove his teeth before he could bite me. I reached the pliers behind me **awkwardly.**

The alligator bit the pliers out of my hand and swallowed them **greedily.**

I was *sure* he would swallow me next. But then I saw the tree. I raced to it and began to climb it **clumsily.**

The alligator was right behind me. He lunged at me, growling **loudly.**

He caught me! My foot was
in his mouth! "I am lost!"
I pulled desperately.

nap!!

And then, my shoe came off. The alligator fell to the ground with my shoe in his mouth. He dropped it. He growled. He prepared to lunge at me again. But then he sniffed the air **painfully.**

He fell on his back. His eyes rolled in his head. He was finished. I climbed down. I picked a flower, and laid it on him gently.

I then put on my shoe and continued on my way to town. I would hurry this time. I would buy some new socks, immediately.

I would throw away my old socks. They were dangerous. And yet, they had saved my life. And for that, I would always remember them . . .